WHAT HAPPENED TO OUR FRIEND MIKEY?

Sean McGrath

This is a work of fiction. Names, characters, and incidents either are the product of the author's imagination or are used fictitiously. Any resemblance to actual persons, living or dead, is, like life itself, entirely coincidental.

Copyright © 2021 by Sean McGrath

All rights reserved. No part of this book may be reproduced or used in any manner without written permission of the copyright owner except for the use of quotations in a book review. For more information, inquiries, or just to say hi, send an email to the author:
sean.mcgrath@live.com

First paperback edition March 2021

Book design by Katarina Naskovski

ISBN 978-0-578-84816-7 (paperback)

INTRODUCTION

THEO [*voiceover*]: We still don't know what happened. Sure, there are innuendo and rumors, questions that fill the vacuum of absence like an octopus, tentacles of speculation reaching every inch of the void until the entirety of "I don't know" is replaced with "Maybe it's this." Then even that discussion splinters into factions of those who want to talk about it, laugh about it, joke about it—maybe using his name as a created answer to a Cards Against Humanity prompt—and those who wish never to speak about it again; a post-traumatic internalized existentialism. And the rest of us, we're left to guess, left to try and figure out how it's possible that our friend Mikey is a murderer. But it's more than that. Criminality is as common as a college degree. It's about the systematic transformation of a beloved friend into a liar, a charlatan, a fraud, a killer, a ghost.

The signs are there, they say. Look hard enough, scrutinize your past, and it's easy to predict these kinds of things. You see what you want to see in someone, reflect what you put out, turning any relationship into a two-way mirror. But there are exceptions. Mikey is this exception. He has to be. Because the alternative means that the four of us were all used, for whatever reason, to abet insanity. And I can't abide that. Because when I look on my own interactions with Mikey, I remember the kid who let me hide out at his house, back in fifth grade, after I bloodied another friend's nose in an afterschool fight. The guy who came to visit me in Madrid for forty-eight hours only to fly back to the States after the weekend was over. The man who reminded me every time we were together of my worth and value as a human being.

"We're all geniuses in our own way, the five of us," Mikey said early one afternoon towards the end of our friendship. "We all have our niches, something we're great at." He named them. "We're experts in our field, and working together, we can change the world, we can change ourselves, we can make society fucking better, man. Isn't that the point?"

But I'm getting ahead of myself.

The old neighborhood was the same. Alright, maybe not exactly the same—nothing can be exactly the same after twenty-five years—but the same type of same as recognizing a person underneath his Halloween costume. The Colombian restaurant wasn't there anymore, but its façade was, and suddenly, there we were. The five of us, kids again, transposed onto the oil stained, wheaten sidewalks asking for change. Panhandling in front of chasing lights and tinted windows. Dickensian pips asking, "May I please have a quarter to call my mom, mister?" Sometimes, we amassed enough to go to Sunnyside Pizza on Greenpoint Avenue and play Street Fighter II until we had no more money. Usually though, we'd head down the street to the Smiles Deli bodega and buy a quarter water each. For whatever reason, we called it "Pal's."

We had the type of relationship with those clerks that only children can have. Their watchful eyes emboldened us; their groans when we entered were a source of humor. Once, Charl and I spent twenty minutes sitting on the floor playing Doggie Doggie Diamond to choose which small bag of potato chips we wanted to take with us. After we got yelled at, we chose Onion Rings. When raves became popular and drugs like ecstasy took over the party scene, Pal's stocked lime green and translucent pacifiers. That summer, we wore them around our necks and in our mouths when we played hockey or basketball or baseball at St. Theresa's around the corner. We never made the connection and, surprisingly, neither did our parents. "Must be a new fad," they probably said.

There was a sense of ownership of the neighborhood that gets lost in adulthood. And at nine and ten years old, walking around the streets with impunity, Jesus, that independence meant something. It still does. Sunnyside was the extended family outside of our own, and we grew up with that security even when something threatened it. Like the time the rumors went around the neighborhood that a maroon van with tinted windows was driving around snatching up children. One day, Marquette and I were across the street from my apartment building, dribbling an underinflated basketball. I never saw the van. But Marquette did. "It's the van! Run!" He shouted. We sprinted back towards the rectory, enveloped in tranquil cotton candy bushes. And Father John was there doing whatever paperwork it was that priests at St. Theresa's did. The van presumably kept rolling down the street.

One autumn, we all got jobs delivering flyers for a new laundromat. The owner paid us $2 an hour. Most of the time, we handed out a couple like we were newspaper boys at the turn of the twentieth century, shouting and hollering about "the best place to get yer clothes cleaned." Once we got bored—usually after twenty minutes or so—

we'd drop the rest of them into one of the metal orange garbage bins stationed at every corner and head off to play basketball. But one weekend close to Halloween, we decided to go to the housing projects on 44th Street. Building by building, we left entire reams scattered along the well-worn octagonal tiles, littering the off-white floors with reams of paper. As we were finishing up in Building 1A, a man—easily a foot taller than any of us—came out of his apartment and demanded we clean up our mess.

Mikey, who had a mouth and a temper, told the guy to go fuck himself. Mikey got punched in the face. Cam stepped in and got in one good right hook before we all ran. That night, our parents drove around the neighborhood looking for the guy. We never found him.

Together, we built Sunnyside in our own image. It was what we needed it to be. Each block was its own little area to explore, each with its own unique smells and sounds. The dueling bells from the Romanian and Greek churches across the street from one another, the car horns, the vroom vroom of the occasional motorcycles, they all had their place. They existed alongside the glottal, terse sounds of Korean, the rolled Rs of Spanish, the fricative sounds of English, each uniquely frozen philological block melting into one discordantly beautiful puddle. And we spoke that language fluently, learning the best places to go for just about anything: Italian ices? That's Sal's Pizza. It was the only place in town with chocolate chip flavor. Fireworks? The Spanish-American Delicatessen on 46th Street will hook you up, but go any further and you're in drug dealer territory. Trying to kiss a girl? The projects on 48th Avenue had recessed alcoves. And our secret spot for watching a basketball game? Climb the fence behind the church parking lot, walk ten steps and climb to the roof of the shed.

And then, just as quickly, it would seem, we'd climb off the shed. The game would end. We would become leaves clinging onto the swaying branch of an autumnal tree not ready to let go. Cam moved first, to Long Island. Then I left; went to Ridgewood with my family. That feeling, that utterly hopeless feeling of unrequested newness, it followed me through eighth grade and into high school, two places where I knew no one and became a completely different person: shy, reserved, unsure. Although Ridgewood was only a fifteen-minute drive away, it felt like the other side of the world, and I never went back to the old neighborhood. I couldn't. It was no longer mine.

Charl, Mikey, and Marquette stayed in Sunnyside and went to high school together but split apart after graduation. By the time college rolled around, I didn't really speak with any of them, and made my own friends at Boston University. I studied communications there, like Howard Stern, hoping that his story would be my own. It didn't work out that way. Instead, I double-majored in creative writing and journalism, interning with local papers up in Massachusetts, before moving to Austin with my girlfriend, Victoria, who got a position in the burgeoning tech industry right out of college.

Charl went to UT Austin and parlayed an internship at the capitol into a congressional staffer position. Mikey started medical school at Dell the same year Charl was a senior, and they reconnected accidentally, as Charl tells it, on separate dates at a fancy Japanese restaurant, the one with the prix fixe menu and tasting sizes, across from the gas station.

Marquette—Marquette University, fittingly enough—moved down to Austin because Charl and I were there, and a random business trip is how Cam (U of A, Roll Tide) helped recreate our crew again. He requested a transfer and it was provided.

And boy did we ever make the city ours. Thirty years of backlogged memories scrambling for a spot in the conversation, sitting astride the comfort of home. Each phrase, said with a smile, delivered with earnestness and joy. There's a fluidity to friendship, real friendship, that doesn't rely solely on shared experiences, but gives space for shared values. That's the kind of family we were. Until we weren't. Until life events and jobs, marriages and mortgages, carried most of us away once more.

I was the first one at The Bar, a low-key dive sitting between a 99¢ Store and a Spanish church. The exterior was tiled over in blue with the alternating rectangular structure of a kitchen backsplash. Gray and earthen bricks endemic to New York City's mid-century construction peeked through the space between the bar and the upstairs apartments. Back when my dad worked here, back when it was called Wayne's, there were two taps: Guinness and Bud Light. Now there are twelve. Craft beers. Chalk drawings of a panda bear holding a eucalyptus leaf and a mug of foam. A pool table. The hanging clouds of smoke that powder my hazy memories replaced by a couple of televisions and a pinball machine. It's certainly an upgrade.

We were here in New York, my request, after seeing the headlines like: WOMAN BLUDGEONED TO DEATH WITH WINE BOTTLE, SUSPECT'S WHEREABOUTS UNKNOWN, and the tweets. Those were hard to scroll through. It was incessant: everyone had a take, and it seems that even more had memes. Police came to our homes, each of us, to ask questions, to pull out information we didn't have. No, we didn't know where Mikey was. Sure, you can search our phones as evidence. Yes, you can follow up with us if you have any further questions. And they did, once or twice. Two in the morning phone calls. I'm assuming it's to catch liars in states of repose, but I knew exactly what they knew, which was exactly what any of us knew. The calls grew more and more infrequent until they stopped, around the same time the story faded from the front pages, turning into little blurbs in areas like the Metropolitan Section of the New York Times, sandwiched next to a feel-good story about an ice cream truck and a cutesy one about love on the rails. And while the press may have decided that there was nothing left to tell, we needed our own closure, and texting from afar was unlikely to bring it to us. It's why we were here.

And when we were all seated, when Cam and Charl and Marquette, when everybody had drinks and dispensed with the hugs, the kisses, the pure joy of being with chosen family, our conversation began.

WHAT HAPPENED TO OUR FRIEND MIKEY?

CHARACTERS

THEODORE SEDJWICK (THEO)
CAMERON KING (CAM)
CHARLEMAGNE MONGELLO (CHARL)
MARQUETTE SHIELDS

SETTING: The Bar, a local bar on 46th Street in the Sunnyside neighborhood of Queens, New York.

TIME: A brisk spring evening in April 2021.

ACT I

9:25 P.M.

When the CURTAIN *rises, we see The Bar is empty save for a couple of regulars: an older man in a worn baseball cap reading the newspaper and eating a slice of pizza. He's seated in the corner closest to the exit. Another man, middle-aged, makes conversation with the young, tattooed bartender. There's a patio out back, but it's closed because of the evening's chill. A KISS pinball machine pressed against the back wall of the bar displays a high score in pixelated orange numbers.*

The four men are seated center stage around a square, wooden table. THEO's *Guinness is half finished.* MARQUETTE *holds a tumbler of whiskey.* CAM *sips a vodka and soda through a thin paper straw, and* CHARL's *Hellbender IPA bubbles up his Bud Light pint glass.*

CHARL: I'm gonna be honest, I really don't know what more there is to talk about. What, we're going to sit here and discuss how he killed [*He lowers his voice.*] his wife? His fucking wife, Theo, and how we're all victims of this, well, this, this, this lunatic, quite frankly? And how we're wrapped up in these investigations... And how I have police calling my house, bothering—

THEO: Still?

CHARL: —my wife and child—yeah, man. Still. They're asking if I've seen Mikey because he once put me down as an emergency contact when he went to a hospital?

THEO: I know, dude. You're right. I love you and you're right. Cops have called all of us.

CAM: Yup.

THEO: I know you have a kid. I know that's an added stressor, and I'm sorry. I am. But I'd like to just talk it through with you all. I want to start from the beginning.

CHARL [*sighing*]: I know. I'm sorry. This still has me on edge.

MARQUETTE: It has us all on edge, dude. But that's why we're here, right?

CHARL: I know, I know. It's—

THEO: It's like... if we start from the beginning, maybe we can, I dunno, get some, like, clues or something?

MARQUETTE: Clues?

THEO: Well, like... okay, Quette, do you remember when you first met Mikey?

MARQUETTE: Not really. I don't remember meeting him because he was always there, just like you guys were always there. Kids in the neighborhood. It's kind of hard to pinpoint a specific instance, where, like, pre-Mikey and post-Mikey intersect. But the summers I can remember, he was there for everything. Manhunt, basketball, that time fuckin', what's his name, Kieran O'Connell, the time he fell out of a tree and needed stitches in his asshole.

CHARL [*laughing*]: Leave it to you, Marquette.

THEO [*laughing*]: Yo.

CAM: Time out.

MARQUETTE: You guys don't remember that?

CAM: No!

MARQUETTE: Yeah, dude. He climbed a tree outside of his apartment and the branch broke. And then—

EVERYONE *laughs.*

[*He continues laughing.*] Then Mikey picked him up and carried him across the street.

CHARL [*suddenly remembering*]: That's right! That's right, Marquette.

MARQUETTE: Kieran was not happy.

CHARL: Neither was his mom.

MARQUETTE: Mikey was, though. It was the first time I remember him saying that he wanted to be a doctor.

Maybe that was the beginning of it, I don't know. There was a pride he had in helping others, of belonging to or doing something outside of himself.

CHARL: It actually, strangely enough, reminds me of the time when… okay, do you guys remember the patch of wood or, like a forest, behind the nursing home?

THEO: Holy shit.

CHARL: You remember this place?

CAM: Yes.

THEO: Of course.

CHARL: Okay. So one day, we all climbed the fence and wandered our way back to this forest.

THEO: But like, it wasn't really a forest, just a bunch of trees?

MARQUETTE: You're describing a forest.

THEO: Yeah, but it—

MARQUETTE: Shut up, dummy, let him talk.

CHARL: Any-way. So we're walking back to the forest and there was this patch of land. Looked like a dried-up puddle, but larger, like mud had pooled. And there was this flat rock, kind of like a tree stump. And at the base of the tree stump were these Hustler magazines.

CAM [*laughing*]: Yup.

CHARL [*after a short pause*]: I mean, that's it. [*He laughs.*] That's the story. I dunno where they came from. I dunno who left them there, but I bring it up because I remember Mikey telling us that we were "officially men" that day.

MARQUETTE [*laughing*]: That's right. He gave that whole speech like, [*He brings a closed fist to his heart.*] "Gentlemen…"

CAM [*speaking along with* MARQUETTE]: "Gentlemen…"

MARQUETTE *and* CAM *laugh.*

CHARL: He wanted it to be our secret, something that we all shared together, like the movies. And I guess, retelling it now, it kind of feels that way doesn't it?

MARQUETTE: In a way.

CAM: If we're talking memories from Sunnyside… y'all remember Delan?

CHARL: That's a name I haven't heard in a while.

THEO: Yeah, scrawny little kid. He picked on me. I think he beat me up once or twice.

CAM: Man, we all beat you up once or twice.

THEO: I was never a good fighter.

CAM: Yeah. [*He playfully hits* THEO *on the arm with the back of his hand.*] You were lucky we were around. Quette, do you remember Delan?

MARQUETTE: Nah, I don't.

CAM: Short dude. Skinny. Probably Italian. Always wearing those black wife beaters.

MARQUETTE: You can describe him all you want, I'm still not gonna remember him. [*He stands up.*] I'll be right back. [*He walks towards the bar.*]

CAM: Alright. Well, Theo, you stole Delan's keys for some reason.

THEO: Oh yeah! I did! [*He laughs.*] I don't remember why though.

CAM: Me neither. But you threw them down the sewer grate, the one we all used to climb into at St. Theresa's.

THEO: I can still smell it. Like low tide. There was black sludge down there and we just, like, happily played in it for some reason?

CHARL: You guys. We played in literal shit. That was actual, literal human fucking shit in that sewer and we climbed down there and kicked around in it. We kicked around human shit.

CAM: Probably why Delan wasn't so happy when Theo threw his keys down there.

THEO: I remember this, but I don't remember what happened next.

CAM: Well, those keys were gone. Absorbed by the darkness. Delan was pissed and says something like, [*He shakes his fist menacingly.*] "I'm gonna give you ten seconds..." So Mikey steps up and says, "Throw the first punch." And ol' dude wasn't sure what to do, so he left because no one wanted to fight Mikey. I'm not even sure if he got his keys back.

CHARL: If they were dredged in shit, maybe they were part of the shitballs we played with the next time we climbed in the fucking sewer, is no one else outraged by this?

CAM *and* THEO *look at one another and roll their eyes.*

MARQUETTE *returns from the bar with four shots of rum. He places them down on the table.*

MARQUETTE: Rum runner?

CHARL, CAM, *and* THEO *have a visible aversion to the question, but take the drinks anyway.*

THEO: You're an asshole.

MARQUETTE: How could I not?

EVERYONE *clinks shot glasses. They take a shot of rum and then look at each other in the eyes.* THEO, MARQUETTE, *and* CHARL *wince with the sting of the alcohol.* CAM *starts coughing.* EVERYONE *laughs and reaches for their drinks as a chaser.*

CAM [*sipping his vodka soda*]: It was me.

MARQUETTE: No shit.

CHARL: Mikey was, like, the only person I knew who loved shots of rum.

THEO: God, just the smell of it reminds me of Maverick's.

CHARL: I know what you mean.

THEO: It's almost like I can, if I close my eyes, see, like, [*He gesticulates.*] a green strobe, flashing dark and light. Like I can feel the pounding of bass within my chest.

CAM: All they'd need to do is play some Avicii.

CHARL: Or Rihanna.

THEO: It was like a glove, you guys.

MARQUETTE: What are you talking about?

THEO: Like, it just fit. Every weekend. Without question. Maverick's on Saturday and book club on Sunday. It was like a glove. Kept us warm and protected and with each other. [*After a short pause, he speaks wistfully.*] I really miss it.

CHARL: I have to say, those days in Austin with you guys were probably the best years of my life. I miss it, too.

CAM: Me too.

MARQUETTE: I mean, of course I do, too. And not just Maverick's. I had never been in a book club before the one with you all. And if I'm being honest, I didn't really like most of the books that we chose, so most of the time I was just sitting there thinking, like, "Okay, let's speed this shit up." Especially because they always just kind of felt like the opening act for whatever TV show or movie we were watching afterwards.

CHARL: I got that feeling, too. It was just about being there with you guys.

MARQUETTE: Although, I just wanna say, for the record, I *did* read them all.

CAM [*putting on a false bravado*]: I ain't read shit.

THEO: Yes you did.

CHARL: I read all of them, too.

THEO: No you didn't.

CHARL: Yes I did. Every one.

THEO: You just read The Intelligent Investor.

CHARL [*defensively*]: Great book. It's a great book.

THEO: That book sucks.

CAM: Yeah, sorry man, that book was terrible.

CHARL: It gives you sound investing advice that is as potent today as it was eighty years ago.

THEO [*talking over* CHARL]: So, did Mikey ever have a book club book?

CHARL [*laughing*]: Fuck you.

MARQUETTE [*after a pause*]: No, he didn't. We all did and then it just kinda stopped.

CAM: And that was the week we were supposed to discuss my book.

THEO: Was that The Stranger?

CAM: *L'Étranger*. Yeah.

THEO: Ooh la la. Here's your discussion: I didn't get it.

MARQUETTE: Nah, me neither.

CAM: I mean, I'm not gonna relitigate it here, but it's basically a novel about indifference to life, and not just showing that indifference in the face of death, or through a murder, but in the very act of living itself. It's my favorite book.

THEO: That seems… relevant.

CAM: Book club was his idea, by the way.

THEO: Mikey's? I thought it was yours.

CAM: Nah. We were texting one day and he asked me if I thought we would all be into the idea of a book club. I said, "Yeah, of course, we're a smart bunch except for Theo." [*He throws his arm around* THEO *affectionately.*] He said he missed the discourse of undergrad and wanted to read and discuss something other than medical textbooks. [*He takes his arm away.*] Low-key, he also wanted to use it as an excuse to cook for us.

THEO: There was always a homey vibe going to his spot. It had this, I dunno, this interesting smell, like a sandalwood candle mixed with the hot oven scent of Christmastime. I can't explain it better than that.

CHARL: I know exactly what you mean.

THEO: Yeah, like, I'll smell that every once in a while, in a restaurant or at home, and it will remind me of Mikey with his apron on, laying some kind of roast on his kitchen island, trying to conceal his smile of, what would you call it? Happiness is too, um—

CHARL: Gratitude.

THEO: Yeah, that's it. Gratitude.

CHARL: He was happy to be there, man. We all were.

MARQUETTE: I honestly don't know how much he actually enjoyed the books we read or the movies we watched. I always felt like he was doing it, like Charl said, because it was an opportunity to spend time with all of us.

CAM: Does that matter?

MARQUETTE: Of course not, it's how I felt, too. Your books all sucked.

EVERYONE *laughs*.

But yeah, he was pretty measured. He spoke matter-of-factly. He definitely was doing the reading. He always had valuable stuff to contribute to the conversation. He did all the things that you would want someone in a book club to do.

CAM: I mean, that's how I remember him as well, Quette. He'd speak after all of us had already spoke. He'd offer up this elaborate, detailed synopsis of the book, and then end with the self-deprecating comments.

CHARL: The "But what the fuck do I know?"

CAM: Exactly.

CHARL: Jules never liked when he did that. She felt he debased himself for laughs.

CAM: I mean, we all kind of did.

THEO: How do you guys remember them together?

MARQUETTE: Him and Jules?

THEO: Yeah.

MARQUETTE: I was the one that introduced them so I think that might have been the thing that made him snap.

THEO, CAM, *and* CHARL *laugh*.

It was after I met Anna, so, early 2013. I invited them to a party at my apartment when I lived with Tom Green.

CAM: Damn, I forgot his last name was Green. That motherfucker was really named Tom Green.

THEO: He had kind of a weird energy, too.

MARQUETTE: Yeah, my Tom Green did. TV Tom Green was… okay, yeah, I guess he was weird, too.

THEO: He was.

MARQUETTE: But my Tom Green always wanted to throw parties and we had to compromise because I wasn't about to deal with that aftermath every Sunday.

CAM: Dude didn't clean up after himself, right?

MARQUETTE: Yeah. He was a slob. There would always be beer cans everywhere. The floor would be sticky, and he'd try and induce me to help him tidy up. I wasn't going to say no because I lived there, too, and didn't want to live in a sty. But every Sunday after a party, like clockwork, I'd get a text from Mikey, "Hey man, need help cleaning up?" And every time I'd tell him, "No, no thank you, it's okay," placating responses like that knowing that if he was sending me that message, he was already at the door ready to lend a hand. It's part of the reason why I wanted to introduce him to Jules. Mikey was loyal and dependable. He was kind. And since Jules had just broken up with her boyfriend, I figured she would appreciate someone like Mikey. I thought they'd hit it off. But I spoke to Jules after that party and she said she didn't like that he was always throwing his money around, buying shots for everyone. He was always flippant about money and she took that as really arrogant. I was like, "Hey, give him another chance, he's not arrogant, he just likes to take care of his friends and he's probably just acting weird because he's nervous and he's into you." So, they went on a second date and got together soon after.

THEO: You guys remember that picture that was hanging up in his bedroom above his bed? It was a pretty old black and white photograph of a man, light-haired, sitting, legs akimbo, looking real sullen, head in his hands—

CHARL: Oh yeah!

THEO: —and lording over him, a woman, pointing her finger at him, scolding him for something, holding a rolling pin, and, you know what, as I'm describing this, in hindsight, that's a really fucked up thing to have bought for him, Cam.

CAM [*laughing*]: That shit was mad funny, though.

CHARL: It *was* really funny, you guys.

MARQUETTE: To be fair, he did get it framed, so maybe he saw some truth in it?

THEO: Or maybe he just wanted to be part of the joke.

CAM: I guess that's how I remember them, though. Mikey was [*He searches for the right word.*] he was obedient. Kind of worn down. Still him, still Mikey, but definitely not as sprightly as he was before they got together.

THEO [*sternly*]: Michael.

CHARL [*sternly*]: Michael.

THEO: Michael, clean up this mess, Michael.

CHARL: Michael, make sure you've done your work, Michael.

MARQUETTE: It wasn't all scolding. There was some, but for a long time they were good.

CAM: He wasn't complaining about it, but that dynamic wasn't something that I would want for my own relationships.

THEO: I don't think any of us would.

CHARL: Jules was hot, though.

MARQUETTE: She was. She also wasn't the bossiest version of herself yet so he could just absorb it. He was so even keeled and mellow that, honestly, I think he was just excited to be with someone as hot as she was. He was definitely punching above his weight class.

CHARL: I do think that we sometimes saw the cracks in their relationship on Sunday nights. Like, there were times, right after we'd shown up, where they were very obviously still pissed at each other and trying to cool off to be chill with us.

THEO: Mm hmm.

CHARL: I even remember seeing her snap at him one or two times as well.

CAM: Jules was definitely more up for a fight.

MARQUETTE: I honestly only remember one time where I saw him get passionate, and it wasn't even about a book, it was the stuff with Woody Allen.

THEO: Yes! I remember that.

CHARL: Was I there for that?

MARQUETTE: I—

THEO: Maybe? I don't know. Cam?

CAM: I don't know what y'all are talking about.

MARQUETTE: Maybe you guys weren't there that week. Anyway, we were watching some Woody Allen movie. I don't remember which one.

THEO: It was *Blue Jasmine.*

MARQUETTE: That's it. And it was at the time when more information was coming out about him abusing his daughter. And the conversation I was referring to—and I think it was a good one—was, can you separate the art from the artist?

CHARL: An excellent question.

MARQUETTE: Definitely. Can you still enjoy Woody Allen movies knowing that he was, and is, an abuser?

CHARL: Absolutely not. I can't watch anything with him in it anymore. Just looking at his face triggers a response in me. I don't know what it is. I can't really describe it, but it's this kind of bubbled up rage.

THEO: Mikey disagreed.

CHARL: What?

THEO: He wasn't necessarily defending Woody Allen, but the argument that he made was sound. Basically, if you take anybody who's created anything culturally significant or worthwhile and you look into their private lives and you judge them based on those private lives, we would never have any art.

CHARL *laughs dismissively.*

Because anyone who's ever created anything was kind of an asshole.

CHARL: Creative geniuses can be very shitty people.

MARQUETTE: Explains why you're so lovely.

THEO: But the heated part of the argument didn't really come from him. Jules got pissed that he was defending Woody Allen.

CHARL: I mean, yeah.

THEO: And you can tell she was kind of holding back because we were still there.

CHARL: What did he say in response?

THEO: He was Mikey, man. He was deferential and apologetic. I think, initially, he was stalwart, kind of throwing it back in her face like, "You wear sweatshop-produced designer handbags, how is that any different?" But ultimately, he backed down and apologized. Said he was wrong in—what did he say— [*using air quotes*] "justifying aberrant behavior because of positive personal attachments." I just don't think the argument was worth it to him. Not many arguments were.

CAM: He never wanted to spend his time arguing. I mean, can you blame him? He was always burning the candle at both ends.

CHARL: He was probably exhausted the entire time.

THEO: He never said anything to us about it.

CHARL: Maybe he valued us more than he valued himself.

MARQUETTE: I think we're assigning a lot to him based on what we know now rather than what we knew then. Maybe he spent his time pillow talking with Jules. Maybe he fucking loved talking about shitty books and watching TV.

CHARL: May be.

THEO: Where did they get engaged again?

CHARL: He did it in his apartment.

THEO: Really?

CHARL: You don't remember this?

THEO: No.

CHARL: Yeah, he baked the ring into one of his strombolis and then when she bit into the slice—

THEO: Oh, right.

MARQUETTE: Good thing she didn't choke on that fucking ring.

THEO: Imagine, though? [*Speaking as Jules*] "Oh, hum de dum, what's this?" [*He mimics having difficulty swallow-*

ing a large object, then finally gets it down, sighing with relief.] "Yum. That's great. Anyone for tea?"

CHARL: That was the day that they saw James Van Der Beek just randomly walking down 6th Street drinking a coffee.

THEO: Oh yeah!

CHARL: And I actually have a picture of them from that day. [*He takes out his phone.*]

CAM: You mean it's not your background?

CHARL: That wouldn't be wise.

MARQUETTE: Why do you still have that?

CHARL [*scrolling through his phone*]: I don't delete pictures, man, you know this. Okay, here it is. [*He shows his phone to the group.*]

THEO: Where's Dawson?

CHARL: He's not in this picture.

THEO: Oh. But he looks happy, Mikey. They look happy.

MARQUETTE: I mean, he wasn't a total sociopath, at least not at that point.

CHARL [*offhandedly*]: I honestly don't know, Quette.

THEO: It was more of a statement of fact than one of surprise because his way of saying something was great or wonderful or awesome or whatever was to make it a question.

MARQUETTE: That's kinda how words work, dummy.

THEO: Right, but like, when he was excited about something, he would almost—I dunno, ask?—maybe that's not the right word either, but I remember him saying things like, "This is cool, right?" or "Well, I'm engaged, that's the thing to do, right?"

CHARL: It's almost like he sought validation because of a very low self-confidence, and as someone who has been a high-functioning depressive, I think it's likely he was as well.

CAM: You saw that even back then?

CHARL: Not as much when it was happening. When it was happening, it was more like, he was the guy who brought the party. I didn't give it much thought.

THEO: I mean… he *did* bring the party, but…

CHARL: But what?

THEO: I dunno, I'm trying to figure out what I want to say. Um. It's just… he brought the party, yes, of course, but he never really *was* the party, you know?

MARQUETTE: I can agree with that.

THEO: Yeah?

MARQUETTE: Yeah. He wanted to keep the party going, but he was never the guy who was, like, first one out there on the dance floor. Think about my wedding; he needed to be cajoled into it.

CHARL: That speech he gave, though.

MARQUETTE: It was the first time—and, honestly, I think only time—I remember seeing him cry.

CHARL: *I* was crying.

MARQUETTE: I was honestly more perplexed at first because he and I never really spent a ton of one-on-one time together aside from a handful of Sundays, so when he got up to speak, I thought it was going to be this nice, short message. But he spoke for eleven minutes.

CHARL: You counted?

MARQUETTE: Anna did.

CHARL: He called that speech 'A Paean of Love.' I was there when he was writing it.

MARQUETTE: I was moved by how much he was moved and how he saw my relationship as kind of a bellwether for his own.

CAM: Then he got drunk.

MARQUETTE: Honestly, if he hadn't gotten drunk at my wedding, it would have been a problem.

CHARL: He tried to bribe the bartender after last call.

CAM: This dude put a hundred down on the bar and was like, "No one has to know."

CHARL [*laughing*]: It kind of reminded me of that weekend in New Orleans when we were eating fried chicken at three in the morning falling asleep in our plates and he was googling drink specials on Frenchman Street.

THEO: He never really liked to sleep, did he?

CAM: Actually, he made a comment during that one summer we went to South Padre together—

THEO: Loved that summer.

CHARL: Yes. Excellent summer.

CAM: Absolutely. It was a great weekend. But he told me one night when he couldn't fall asleep that it was because he was a "super sleeper."

CHARL: A what?

CAM: He said he had a "different circadian rhythm" than most people and he only needed one or two hours of sleep per night.

CHARL: Is that a thing?

CAM: I obviously looked it up. Apparently, it is. Though not to the extent that he claimed and certainly not to the extent we'd experience later.

CHARL: Interesting.

MARQUETTE: I'd never heard that.

THEO: I remember you told me that while we were there, Cam. And I thought it was kind of strange at the time, but it never really changed the fact that for me, that summer was, like, the epitome of being young and carefree with your friends. When we all went skinny dipping that night, it was Mikey, usually so reserved and shy when it came to nudity, who just dropped trou and sprinted towards the ocean. And we followed, screaming into the darkness. Laughing. Jesus, it's like… in my mind, it's like a postcard, you know? Silhouettes of our backs against, like, this orange backdrop in that golden hour before sunset.

CHARL: I remember that.

CAM: It was midnight.

THEO: No, I know it was, but in my mind, that's how we all were. We were free.

CHARL: Wow.

THEO: But there's a sadness to it all. Not just because of Mikey but because of time and meaning.

CAM: That's been a universal lament since history started, though. Camus argued that our inability to know, for certain, the meaning of life, should itself be embraced as the meaning of life.

CHARL: Was that in <u>The Stranger</u>?

CAM: In fact, it was.

MARQUETTE: Anyone want another drink? I'll go grab this round.

CAM: Nah, I lost rum runner. Put it on my card. [*He hands* MARQUETTE *his credit card.*]

9:45 P.M.

There's a general clamor of noise throughout The Bar as a number of new customers have come inside. "Jeremy" by Pearl Jam plays over the speakers from the jukebox next to the bar, the one with the bright blue lights along the perimeter. MARQUETTE returns with four beers and puts them on the table while the guys are in the middle of a conversation.

CHARL [*responding to* CAM]: …I wouldn't go out of my way to watch Saved by the Bell. That doesn't mean that it's bad, it's just not critically acclaimed.

THEO [*taking a sip of beer*]: You guys wanna know what else wasn't critically acclaimed?

CHARL: Don't do it.

THEO [*smacking his lips and returning his beer to the table, smiling*]: Mikey's first wedding.

CHARL: Goddammit. Why? Why when we were having such an important conversation?

THEO: Seemed as good a time as any.

CAM: I'm honestly surprised he went through with it.

MARQUETTE: Honestly, I don't recall seeing a "bad version" of Mikey until that night.

CAM: Yeah.

MARQUETTE: I was kind of disappointed not to be a groomsman.

THEO: I wasn't a groomsman either.

MARQUETTE: Yeah, but I introduced them.

THEO: Sure.

MARQUETTE: And this seems like a lie from Mikey—the first that I really remember him saying—but he said that Jules didn't want me to be a groomsman.

CHARL: Really?

MARQUETTE: Yeah.

CAM: I'd never heard this.

MARQUETTE: It's bullshit. And it has to be. Because she and I were friends. We never had any rifts at all.

THEO: But why would he lie about that, though?

CHARL: It's Mikey, man.

THEO: Yeah, but then. Mikey then. "My word is my bond," Mikey. Why would he have lied about that?

CAM: To cover his ass, probably.

THEO: Doesn't make sense that none of us were groomsmen.

CHARL: I was supposed to be.

THEO: What? You never said this.

CHARL: I never told you this?

THEO: No.

CHARL: I must have.

CAM: What happened?

CHARL: He said he wanted to go with just family but he only had one spot available and that it was between me and one of his friends from med school.

MARQUETTE: Uh huh.

CHARL: And it was either sit in the church with you guys or stand up there with his family. And I had never met his family, so I declined.

MARQUETTE: What'd he say?

CHARL: Just that he understood. That was pretty much it. But I was surprised, quite frankly, that his cousins were groomsmen, because I don't ever remember him talking about them. And I thought it was strange that he didn't ask any of you.

MARQUETTE: I didn't care. I wasn't excited about a church wedding to begin with.

CAM: That's what always threw me.

MARQUETTE: On the plus side, I was sitting so far back, I couldn't tell that he was blackout when he was up there. I only heard about it—

THEO: Whoa.

MARQUETTE: —after the fact.

THEO: He was blackout at the altar?

CAM: He *was* slurring his words during the ceremony now that you mention it.

THEO: I hadn't really noticed that.

MARQUETTE: Yeah. Plus, there was that whole "praise Jesus," call-and-response thing that he hadn't agreed to beforehand, which kind of vilified her after their divorce.

THEO: I just assumed he loved her enough to, you know, to, what would you call it? Sacrifice his non beliefs? That sounds stupid.

CAM: I know what you mean.

CHARL: That was the first instance I ever thought something was wrong with him. But at this point, I was obviously more concerned than anything.

MARQUETTE: He didn't speak at the reception either because he was wrecked.

CHARL: When did he pass out in the bathroom?

THEO: What?

CHARL: Uh, yeah, dude.

THEO: How did I not hear about this?

MARQUETTE: Yeah, one of his cousins came over to me and was like, "Yo, can you come help Mikey, he's not doing too hot." And there were about five or six of us who propped him up. He staggered on his own volition to a chair. I asked him if everything was okay. He looked at me glassy-eyed and said, "I'm married," or "I'm married now," or something like that. Then he just fell asleep again.

THEO: Damn. Did you find Jules?

MARQUETTE: Well, yeah. She was crying her eyes out.

THEO: What a baby.

CHARL: Stop.

MARQUETTE: There was no way for her to hide her sadness. Everyone saw him and it was really embarrassing for her. I felt terribly.

CHARL: The next day, people were trying to force him to apologize to her parents.

CAM: Well yeah.

CHARL: There was a sit down where they blamed his behavior on "latent alcoholism" and from being "a lower social caste" than they were.

THEO: These are quotes?

CHARL: These are quotes.

THEO: They said—

CHARL: "A lower—

CHARL AND THEO: Social. Caste."

CHARL: Yup.

THEO: That's horrid.

CHARL: Yup.

THEO: And they used the term "latent alcoholism"?

CHARL: Mm hmm.

THEO: Who told you all this?

CHARL: Mikey did, later on.

THEO: Was he an alcoholic, though?

MARQUETTE: Nah. We'd know if he was. He just liked drinking.

THEO: What's the difference?

MARQUETTE: He didn't do it every day. He didn't, like, wake up and crack open a beer to start his day. He really only drank socially.

CAM: Y'all know I saw Jules at their apartment the next weekend?

CHARL: Nah.

THEO: Really?

CAM: Mikey wasn't there. He was, I think, with his parents or doing residency tours? Do you do residency tours?

CHARL: They just place you at a hospital.

CAM: Then he must have been with his parents. So I go over there—

THEO: You fuck her.

CAM: I don't fuck her.

THEO: That's good, you shouldn't fuck your friends' wives.

CAM: I had no idea she had already filed for divorce.

CHARL: Wait, a week after?

CAM: Yup. She told me she had already filed for divorce but that they still had their honeymoon to go on and they had paid some ridiculous number, like $50,000, to fly to Fiji and Vanuatu, I think, and a bunch of islands near Australia, and she didn't wanna cancel the reservations.

THEO: Holy shit.

CHARL: So they went on their honeymoon with her knowing their divorce was imminent?

CAM: So far as I know.

CHARL: She didn't know he was about to Irish exit the honeymoon, too.

THEO: Oh fuck. He did.

CAM: Yeah, he booked an emergency flight two days after landing in Tahiti and came back home.

THEO: Just the idea of being like, "Well, it's getting late, time to hit the hay," and then sneaking out to drive to the airport and get on a plane. It's absurd.

CHARL: It's insane.

THEO: So how did we justify it?

CHARL: Honestly, I didn't.

THEO: Yes you did.

CAM: We all did.

MARQUETTE: I justified it easily: it's a personal decision that had nothing to do with me.

CAM: Let's be real, here. We blamed her.

THEO: We did blame her.

CHARL: Well, if he truly didn't know anything about the wedding set-up beforehand, which I doubt is true now, then it would make sense that we'd blame her.

THEO: I never bought them anything for the wedding.

CHARL: I did.

CAM: I bought them a set of silverware.

MARQUETTE: You got it back, right?

CAM: Yeah, along with a note that had a really resentful tone.

THEO: I mean—

CAM: I'm just saying, it clearly wasn't written by him.

CHARL: I got a note, too.

MARQUETTE: Mine was more of a memo.

CAM: But that was the last time I ever heard from her.

THEO: She just cut us all out after the wedding.

MARQUETTE: "Cut us all out" is a weird way to phrase that.

THEO: How would you phrase it?

MARQUETTE: All of us were Mikey's friends first, so—

CHARL: She unfriended all of us on social media.

MARQUETTE: I don't really put that on her, though. What was she supposed to do? It was the only option she had.

CAM: I know if Martina and I ever divorced, I sure as hell would unfollow her and all her friends. I don't wanna see their faces while I'm packing my shit up in boxes and moving in with one of y'all.

THEO: There's always a place on our couch for you, buddy.

CAM: I ain't sleepin' on no couch. Give me that queen-sized Casper mattress y'all be laying on all night. You take the damn couch.

THEO [*laughing*]: It's my house.

CAM [*laughing with faux indignancy*]: So?

MARQUETTE: I don't think it's fair to vilify Jules for their relationship.

CHARL: There's not always someone to blame. Just because there's a wrong doesn't mean that only one person is responsible for that wrong, ya know?

MARQUETTE: We can only really know what we saw with our own two eyes. And anything we were told afterwards from Mikey doesn't necessarily mean that what we got was the truth. It also doesn't mean that he was lying.

THEO: It's why evidence is so hard to corroborate, especially when you get an account from someone who is telling you what happened.

CHARL: Right.

CAM: That shit rocked him, though.

THEO: Yeah, I had lunch with him shortly after his honeymoon—if you could call it that—maybe a week or two after he came back and he joked about being divorced. He was like, "Yeah, sometimes it doesn't work out," kind of flippantly.

CHARL: He was probably embarrassed and that's how he knew how to handle it.

THEO: Sure. I'm almost certain that was the case, too. I just wish he were more open about how he was feeling in the moment.

MARQUETTE: But he never was, though. He never really shared what was on his mind. He didn't talk just to talk. In fact, I don't recall an instance where he was like, "Hey guys, I'm feeling kind of sad or down or mad or whatever." It was just a constant even-keel, steady, "this too shall pass" façade.

CAM: Think about it: it's likely he was already checked out of the relationship and, for whatever reason, couldn't bring himself to do anything about it.

CHARL: We've been over why. Admitting there's a problem takes a lot of emotional energy, and Mikey was never really willing to expend that energy. Easier to, I dunno, suppress it?

MARQUETTE: He didn't really suppress—

CHARL: Not suppress, not suppress. Um…

THEO: Push through?

CHARL: Sure. Yeah. Push through. Emotions are hard, man.

MARQUETTE: That relationship, though—the tail end of it anyway—the wedding, the ceremony, and the divorce? Those were all catalysts for the version of Mikey that, you know, that came after.

CAM: When he lost Jules and that home life that he always wanted—

CHARL: He *did* always want that.

CAM: But that's kind of what drove him to double up on classes. He filled his days nonstop. Every hour was scheduled. Did he ever show you his calendar?

THEO: He was over-compensating in many ways.

CHARL: Uh, yeah. He was back in his old apartment, he—

THEO: Wait, where did *she* go?

MARQUETTE: I think she moved back to California.

CAM: Cut her losses and ran.

CHARL: Would you stick around?

CAM: Absolutely not.

CHARL: But then we just stopped seeing a lot of him.

MARQUETTE: Chalk that up to embarrassment, too. You have your best friends at a, what, a $250,000 wedding—

CAM: Yup.

THEO: I'm sorry, a what?

CHARL: Easily that much. Probably more.

THEO: Damn.

MARQUETTE: —and a month later you're alone in the same apartment you shared with your ex-fiancée, you're not even halfway through med school, you owe a huge amount of debt, and you're certainly ashamed about literally everything that had happened. I'd likely hide, too.

THEO: We reached out to him enough, right? I feel like we did.

CAM: We definitely did. All the group texts, "Mikey, we're going to Maverick's," "Mikey, come over for a video game night." We got those short responses, "Can't tonight, studying," "Sorry, I'm busy," "Maybe another time."

MARQUETTE: I even went over there a couple times to try and get him to talk, but he never answered the doorbell.

CHARL: I did, too.

CAM: So there's not much you can do about all that.

MARQUETTE: And then he moved to Houston.

THEO: His goodbye party was… did you guys see anything
wrong then?

CHARL: Not really, but again, I wasn't looking for it. He
seemed fine.

MARQUETTE: That's what I remember about the party. It
was at your spot, Theo.

THEO: Yup. Because Mikey already had his stuff in boxes.

MARQUETTE: And he was just, yeah, he was fine. Regular
Mikey. Shots of rum. Pats on the back.

CAM: He did stay till the end.

MARQUETTE: Before he Irish exited.

CHARL: Yeah, but that was expected. And aside from not
wanting to talk about the wedding, he was, yeah, he
was fine.

THEO: He ate—I had a whole pound cake from Whole
Foods that he just divebombed into at the end of the
night. It was his going-away cake, and he tore it up.
Crumbs all over his face, on the floor. Mouth full, he
was like, [*He mimics having a mouth full of cake.*]
"Thanks buddy." Then he disappeared.

CAM: The next time I heard from him—

MARQUETTE: When we all heard from him?

CAM: Yeah, was that group text, like, two months later.

THEO: January.

MARQUETTE: Right. He had really gotten into gambling. Gambling and stocks. And—

CHARL: He probably read <u>The Intelligent Investor</u>.

THEO: Unlikely.

MARQUETTE: And he… yeah, this is when those texts started, Cam.

CHARL: Which ones?

MARQUETTE: The investment ones.

THEO: And the ones where he'd try to get us to go in on strange political bets with him.

CHARL: Oh shit!

MARQUETTE: Yup.

CHARL: Dude! That shit was so weird. I had never heard Mikey talk much about politics—or investing!—and suddenly I'm getting a call at two in the morning asking me if I wanted to parlay the Portuguese presidential election with the outcome of the Lakers game?

THEO: Did you do it?

CHARL: What? No, c'mon, man.

CAM: The texts I got were a bit erratic. They had an insider trading vibe.

MARQUETTE: Really?

CAM: Yeah. They were manic. There was always a timeline for purchase. I remember having a conversation with him, and he was kind of talking in code, it seemed. He was manipulating his words so that he wasn't saying what he actually meant. And that was never like him. Mikey always said what he meant even if he didn't always share how he felt.

THEO: Things only got worse when he met Susanna.

CHARL: That's the cliff, if we're talking about behaviors that weren't quite right, I think we, [*He stammers.*] I, I, I can… it just kinda shoots off from here.

MARQUETTE: Yeah. There's definitely a Houston Mikey and an Austin Mikey.

THEO: So let's talk about Houston.

CHARL: Ho' boy. I'll need some food for this.

MARQUETTE: I'm pretty hungry, too.

THEO: Alright, I'll go grab some slices from the pizza place down the street. Anyone wanna come with?

CHARL: Actually, yeah, I'll come with you.

MARQUETTE: Cool. I'll stick around and hold our spot.

—The CURTAIN falls

ACT II

10:30 P.M.

When the CURTAIN *rises,* CAM *and* MARQUETTE *are seated having a silent conversation. A couple of people wait patiently at the bar for their orders. Billy Joel's "River of Dreams" plays faintly over the speakers.* THEO *and* CHARL *enter stage right.* CHARL *is holding a box of pizza with a cartoon of a smiling Italian chef on the top. More than one person asks, "Is that for me?" as* THEO *and* CHARL *walk past bar patrons and put the pizza down on the wooden table. There are new beers in each of the four positions. The men each take a slice of pizza from the box and close it.*

THEO: So. Houston Mikey. [*He takes a bite.*]

CHARL: Uh huh…

THEO [*offhandedly*]: This is so fucking good. Jeez. I missed New York pizza.

CHARL [*taking a bite*]: Dude. I know.

THEO: What, um, where do—okay, so—

MARQUETTE: That's a good point. Anyone else?

THEO: I can't really figure out what I'm trying to say.

MARQUETTE: How long after he moved to Houston did he meet Susanna?

CHARL: They were working at the hospital together, but I don't think it was immediate. I remember him texting me about her, telling me that he liked her but he wasn't sure if that sort of thing was frowned upon or not.

CAM [*motioning with his slice of pizza*]: Now was this before or after he said he was dating Gigi Hadid?

CHARL: Jesus.

MARQUETTE: No, that was after they broke up but before they got back together.

CAM: Just… I can't—

MARQUETTE: Didn't he say his broker set them up?

CHARL: Something like that, yeah.

THEO: Wasn't she with Zayn at the time?

CAM: Well that's why he said they didn't have sex.

CHARL: "Too much respect" for Zayn to do that.

THEO: He told me she invited him up but he declined because he had work.

CAM: Bullshit.

CHARL: Of course it's bullshit.

THEO: I actually believed him.

CHARL: No.

THEO: Yeah. Imagined myself in his position, at the foot of a high-rise.

CHARL: Stop.

THEO: The lingering moments after the date ends but before it's over.

CHARL: No, Theo, really?

THEO: Yeah, dude. I thought back to the GQ magazine I had with her in it.

CAM: The one you jerked off to.

THEO: When your mother wasn't available.

CHARL: Wait, Theo, you're not joking?

THEO: No.

CHARL: You actually believed him?

THEO: Why wouldn't I?

CHARL: Because it's weird and it's implausible and it's so easily disproven.

THEO: Sure. You're not wrong. But maybe I saw a potential future for myself, ya know? Mikey definitely punched up with Jules and Gigi was an elevator to the top. So if *Mikey* could land someone like Gigi…

CHARL: Oh, you were lonely.

THEO: Not lonely, just looking for hope where none actually existed.

MARQUETTE: I want to go on record as saying that I kind of believed it as well. At least for a little bit.

CHARL: You, Quette?

MARQUETTE: I believe all my friends. And Mikey really hadn't had a track record of dishonesty at this point, so when someone I consider family tells me something, no matter how wild or out there it seems, I gotta go with my first instinct. And in this case, my first instinct was to... yeah, was to be jealous of him.

CHARL: I can understand that.

CAM: There wasn't a small part of you that believed him?

CHARL: Me? No, man. It's not that I didn't trust him at the time, but... you guys, Gigi Hadid lives in California. How could— his broker set them up? Like, I didn't... it never made sense to me.

THEO: Did you ever call him out on it?

CHARL: At the time? No. I just kinda laughed about it with Portia.

CAM: What'd she say?

CHARL: You know Portia, she's trusting but skeptical. At first, she thought he was telling the truth, but then when we did some googling, there was no way any of it was true. But I *had* planned on confronting him when I went to go visit.

THEO: Weren't we all there?

CHARL: No, we all went during the summer, when we went to the Astros game. This isn't that time. I went about a month after he moved down to help him get settled in his new place.

MARQUETTE: Oh, right, that was the weekend I went to visit my sister for her birthday.

CAM: You stay overnight?

CHARL: Yeah, but not with him. We just spent the afternoon together. Left early, took the car up, stopped by his place. Hung out. He had patients to attend to during his evening shifts and said I could stay, but I didn't really want to be there when he wasn't. [*He pauses.*] I feel like I kind of repressed this memory because it was so strange, but we went to a place called Potente.

CAM: Really?

CHARL: You know that place?

CAM: Yeah. It's expensive as hell.

CHARL: It *was* expensive as hell. But Mikey was all, "I got this, you're my guest, I'll take care of it."

CAM: As he does.

CHARL: Right. As he does. So, we're catching up at the restaurant, I'm telling him about my job down here, about you guys, the usual banter. He's telling me about rotations, how difficult they are. Pretty standard stuff.

But then he says the weirdest shit I've heard, possibly in my entire life.

THEO: What? What'd he say?

CHARL: Well, after our normal conversation, he brought up another "investment opportunity." I think it was real estate this time. Doesn't matter. I was like, "No, Mikey, I actually don't have the money to be investing right now. I have a kid and money's a little tight."

THEO: Okay.

CHARL: Then he gets close to me, like uncomfortably close. [*He leans in.*] Closer than we are now. And his voice gets real low. Like he's whisper talking. He tells me that he has to keep the tips a secret because people were listening in on our conversations and that we had to whisper because the hospital had plants assigned to him.

CAM: Um.

THEO: He was joking, right?

CHARL: No, man. He's never joked around like that. This was a different level.

THEO: Plants?

CHARL: Like operatives. People who were working for the hospital to spy on him.

THEO: What? Why didn't you tell us that when you came back?

CHARL: I dunno, I didn't really want to think about it, I guess.

MARQUETTE: That *is* weird.

THEO: Seems like drugs to me.

CHARL: I've never known Mikey to take drugs—or I guess I hadn't at that point.

MARQUETTE: He did used to joke about needing cocaine to focus. Which, is that what cocaine does?

CAM: It can.

CHARL: It's got a similar chemical composition to speed, so I guess, yeah.

THEO: He once mentioned to me, when we were in his house, I guess it was that summer? He said, "Don't go in my bedroom unless you want to want to see what $147,000 in prescription drugs looks like."

CHARL: What?

THEO: Yeah. It was weird. I was just like, "Ha ha, okay, Mikey," and laughed it off. At the time, I wasn't sure if he was serious or not, but now I'm kind of convinced he was.

CHARL: The strangest part of the whole thing is that he never brought it up again. Usually with jokes you kind of replay them, run them into the ground.

MARQUETTE: Some of us have new material.

CHARL: Not me. [*He laughs.*] But yeah, he never brought it up again. Not with me, and I guess never with you all either.

THEO AND MARQUETTE: Nope.

CAM: Damn.

THEO: How did you guys feel about the weekend we spent there?

CAM: *The* weekend.

THEO: Right. *The* weekend.

MARQUETTE: I don't—I guess he looked the same.

CHARL: Sure. It had only been six months since we all saw him, he's not going to look that different.

THEO: Yeah, but there was something—

CAM: Weird?

THEO: —off. Yeah, weird's a good way to put it.

MARQUETTE: This is all hindsight.

CHARL: Sure, but it's hard to tell a story absent of it.

MARQUETTE: I think we're better than that.

CAM: You can call something weird even if we didn't fully grasp the extent of it at the time.

MARQUETTE: What specifically are you referring to?

CAM: Fabolous.

MARQUETTE: Oh fuck. I forgot about Fabolous.

THEO: I remember thinking it was one of those things that's so outrageous, that it can't possibly be a lie. You know, kind of like Gigi Hadid.

CAM: Theo, you really believed ol' dude wrote the album Loso's Way? The entire album?

THEO: He said he used the pen name, oh shit what was it?

MARQUETTE: Rico Street.

CHARL: No, that wasn't it. Close, but that wasn't it.

CAM: Street Law, Rico Law, something like that.

THEO: Rico Law! That's it! And, dude, you try looking up Rico Law on Wikipedia—and believe me, I did, I have, and I continue to—there's no page for him.

CHARL: Because he's a low-level producer from the 2000s, man.

THEO: But isn't it possible—

CHARL: Absolutely not. We were all in college then, dude. And I'm certain that Fabolous wasn't searching for college-aged students from fucking DePaul University especially when—

THEO: Where is Fabolous from?

CAM AND CHARL: Brooklyn.

CHARL: And, Theo, Mikey doesn't write music. That's—

THEO: Not that we've seen.

CHARL: —crazy. No, Theo, no. You can't be so naïve, especially when put up against literally everything else that happened afterwards. I know you love these memories of Mikey, man—

THEO [*interrupting*]: Loved.

CHARL: No, love. Current. It's hard to stop loving someone, especially someone you've known for thirty years. That doesn't just go away. But part of love is that critical analysis that's so crucial to understanding one another. And it's hard because it was in the middle of a typical conversation, the same ones we've had hundreds of times, so when you sandwich in a blatant lie between blatant truths, that lie becomes that much harder to debunk.

THEO: Am I naïve?

CAM: Yes.

MARQUETTE: You're trusting. You're a good, kind person who sees the best in everyone. And the thing with Mikey was that he was always the guy who would stand up to liars and bullies. His credibility lay in his pursuit of the truth.

CHARL: Dude, there was a time in high school where Mikey called out a teacher for wearing an NRA t-shirt.

MARQUETTE: Mr. Hammerschmidt.

CHARL: Mr. Fuckin' Hammerschm—you remember that guy?

MARQUETTE: I never had him. But I remember him and the smug look he had trouncing down the hallways looking like Bill from Guess Who.

CHARL: Holy shit, Quette. That's amazing.

CAM: This dude wore an NRA shirt to school and still had a job?

CHARL: Tenure, man.

CAM: True.

CHARL: But Mikey called him out one day. He came into class with that dumbass shirt on and Mikey raised his hand, calmly—and keep in mind, this was only a couple years after Columbine—and said something like, "How dare you bring your dangerous gun worshipping bullshit into our school?" I don't know if that was the exact quote, but it was something that called those gun nuts out on their hypocrisy.

THEO: Did he get put out?

CHARL: Of course he got put out. Hammerschmidt sucked, dude. But Mikey never got in trouble and I didn't see Hammerschmidt wear that shirt anymore.

THEO: Dope.

CHARL: Point being, you're right, Marquette. Mikey was always credible. Which is why, Theo, I think you're still, even now, having a hard time reconciling the person you knew him to be with the person he is. Or the person he became.

CAM: And it wasn't even Fabolous' best album.

CHARL [*laughing*]: It certainly wasn't.

CAM: But then the next day was great.

CHARL: All-time great day.

CAM: Home plate seats at the Astros. Steak dinner.

THEO: Fantasies.

CAM: You loved Fantasies, didn't you?

THEO: Strip clubs aren't usually my thing, but I really liked Fantasies.

CAM: You just liked the lap dances Mikey bought for you.

THEO: That… may have been part of it, yeah.

CAM: Yo, but were his bets really paying off like that, though?

CHARL: He showed me his portfolio at the game. He had over a million dollars available to trade.

THEO: Christ.

MARQUETTE: I'm sorry, did you say a million?

CHARL: A million four, actually.

MARQUETTE: Maybe I should have gotten in on that insider trading.

THEO: Shh… there are plants here.

CHARL: He paid the stripper $15,000 that night, too.

CAM: What?

CHARL: He was gone for over an hour and [*He laughs.*] honestly, it was just like *Hustlers*. He was wrecked when he came back, his hair was ruffled, his shirt was untucked.

MARQUETTE: Huge smile on his face.

CAM: Came out of that champagne room lookin' like he drank all the champagne.

MARQUETTE: Maybe he did.

THEO: It'd explain why he slept through breakfast.

CHARL: And lunch.

CAM: Well, we left before then.

THEO: And then—

CHARL: What do you mean?

THEO: Then we didn't hear from him.

MARQUETTE: And then nothing.

THEO: Radio silence for, what, four months?

CAM: It wasn't all radio silence, he just stopped responding to texts.

MARQUETTE: Most texts.

CHARL: And phone calls.

CAM: Right, and phone calls.

CHARL: And my wedding.

THEO: Yeah, what the fuck, dude? That whole story…

CHARL: And the fucking nerve to blame me for being upset.

CAM: Whoa. He blamed you?

CHARL: Yeah, man. The next day at breakfast, he called me, apologetic, said he couldn't switch his shift in time, then t—

THEO [*interrupting*]: Whoa, wait. Hold up.

CHARL: What?

THEO: He told you that he couldn't switch his shift?

CHARL: Yeah, why?

THEO: Uh oh.

CHARL: What?

THEO: He texted me when we were all having breakfast. Lemme find it. [*He takes out his phone, unlocks it, and starts scrolling.*]

MARQUETTE: I actually hadn't heard anything from him. I heard why he didn't show up from Portia. I'm not sure how she found out, though. Did you tell her, Charl?

CHARL: Yeah, of course.

CAM: Portia told me, too. She pulled me aside during breakfast—so maybe that was after—

THEO: Okay, here it is. Sorry. [*He reads from his phone.*] "Hey, dude, can you do me a favor? Please tell Charl I'm sorry, I got detained for drunk driving. It was a stupid mistake. I'll never do it again. The police kept me overnight in a cell (in case you're wondering what a holding cell smells like: it's piss. The movies are right). I'm home now and am going to make it up to him. I already called him myself, but another sorry coming from you would mean a lot and will calm the waters until I get to see him in person. Thanks, buddy."

CHARL: Dude. What the fuck?

THEO [*sheepishly*]: He said you knew, so, like, there was no real use, I guess, in relaying the entire message?

CAM: What? Shit. Yo, that's so irresponsible.

MARQUETTE: Fuck, dude. That's so fucking selfish.

CHARL: Hold on. I'm sorry, I can't get over this. I feel like a can of paint is on my chest. Theo, he literally told you why he wasn't at my wedding and then told me a completely different story?

THEO [*hesitantly*]: Yeah.

CHARL: I don't—I can't und—I'm gonna need a minute. [*He stands up and walks away from the table.*]

THEO [*after a moment of silence*]: Fuck. Guys, I feel awful. Should I have shared the entire message with him?

CAM: I mean, yes? But also, he specifically told you in that message that Charl already knew, so I can see why you'd just share what he asked you to.

MARQUETTE: I wouldn't worry about it.

THEO: I don't want Charl to be upset with me. Like, I just assumed he knew because Mikey said he knew.

MARQUETTE: Charl's just sensitive, dude. You know how he can get. He'll be fine.

CHARL *returns to the table.*

CAM: You good? You need some water?

CHARL: I got some, thanks. [*He sighs.*] It's like the moment after a jump scare in a horror film.

THEO: I feel awful, dude. I should have showed you the whole text. I have no idea why I didn't do it back then. I'm so sorry.

CHARL: What? No, man. I'm not mad at *you*. There was literally no reason for you to think that anything he told you wasn't true.

THEO: Yo. Wait. What if what he told me wasn't true?

CHARL: What do you mean?

CAM: Why would he make up a story about drunk driving and being arrested?

THEO: Because it's more plausible when it comes to missing a wedding than absentmindedness?

MARQUETTE: Alright, hold up. Did he even have a car?

CHARL [*after a pause*]: No…

THEO: How far away is the hospital from his apartment?

CAM: What was the address?

CHARL: It's about an hour walk.

CAM: He coulda used Uber or metro, though.

THEO: Mikey'd never use public transport. Of all the options presented, he'd pick the most expensive one.

CAM: Uber's expensive.

CHARL: So's renting a car.

THEO: Shit.

MARQUETTE: So what are our options? None of them good, by the way. Either Mikey rented a car, drove drunk, was detained and missed the wedding, or he didn't rent a car, lied about driving drunk, and missed the wedding.

THEO: And, like, fuck, you guys, I don't associate with people who drive drunk so I'm kind of kicking myself for ignoring it "because it's Mikey," you know.

MARQUETTE: It's easy to give friends passes on things because you know them, or you think you know them.

CAM: It's like any relationship that you have where you project your feelings about the other person onto them because you want to consider yourself a good judge of character.

CHARL: I still can't believe he missed my wedding. I felt like such an idiot having to explain to my family and to Portia's family that he wasn't coming because he couldn't get off work. *And* he was a groomsman.

MARQUETTE: I don't know if it'll make you feel better, but I don't think anyone really noticed. Portia only had four bridesmaids, so it kind of worked out well.

CAM: For what it's worth, I didn't hear anyone mention Mikey.

CHARL: It's not the point.

CAM: No, I know.

CHARL: For my family and her friends to hear me talk about what a great guy Mikey is and how he's one of my oldest friends and then for him to just not show up, I felt like a total asshole.

MARQUETTE: I know man. And then we spent that year afterwards trying to get everything back to where it was.

CAM: Crazy that we spent that long.

MARQUETTE: He was a friend, dude. And if he needed help, like we assumed he did later on, it's kind of on us to help him.

CHARL: You're so good, Marquette.

MARQUETTE: It's not about being good, it's about loyalty to your friends—family—and saying, "Hey, if you need help, we got you."

CAM: He never asked for help, though.

MARQUETTE: All the more reason to give him a shoulder to lean on.

THEO: But, like, during that time, man, his paranoia became—

CAM: It was off the charts.

THEO: Comical.

CHARL: It would have been comical if it didn't directly impact our lives.

MARQUETTE: Shortly after your wedding, Charl, I remember a text from him asking me if I liked my job. I think he phrased it like, "Are you satisfied in your career?" And I wasn't, of course. I didn't want to be a data analyst forever.

CHARL: Didn't you just watch movies at that job?

MARQUETTE: I saw all three Die Hards in one shift. That was a busy day.

CHARL: Oh my God.

MARQUETTE: Then there was the month I watched every Bond movie. God, some of them are truly awful.

CHARL [*laughing*]: No, they don't all hold up.

MARQUETTE: So, "being satisfied" in my job is a tricky question, because, no, career-wise, I wouldn't be making the money I am now if I had stayed with that bullshit company, but I also watch significantly fewer Bond movies, so…

CHARL: Priorities.

MARQUETTE: But I bring it up because—and I'm pretty sure I told you guys this—but he told me he could get me a job at Baylor.

CAM: I'm pretty sure he told all of us that.

MARQUETTE: And I texted back like, "No thanks, I don't have medical experience and I don't like hospitals." So he called me and spoke for about an hour straight about how I didn't even need to set foot in the hospital, how I was going to make a six-figure salary, how the university—which is where I would have been working—could use my expertise to craft a more comprehensive, fuckin', patient care system or some shit. I don't know. But—

CHARL: Dude, he told me the same thing. But he said that he actually went ahead and got me an interview with the president of Baylor. I think it was his way of apologizing for missing my wedding.

THEO: You didn't go?

CHARL: Of course I didn't go. I work at the capitol, why the hell would I want to move to Houston to work in medicine?

MARQUETTE: He wouldn't take no for an answer.

CHARL: And what's strange is that the day I was "supposed" to go in, I just no showed. I never got an email, phone call, nothing, either from him or from the president about not showing up.

THEO: Well, they likely had a lot of candidates for the position. They're a big school.

CHARL: Dude. There was no position.

THEO: What?

CHARL: Yeah, dude. He made it up. No position. No interview. No president.

THEO: Really?

CHARL: Think about it. How would a doctor—not even a doctor, a trainee, someone on rotation—have access to the fucking president of one of the most respected medical schools in America?

THEO: Unless he made a name for himself working stocks there?

CHARL: A million-dollar portfolio isn't going to raise any eyebrows, especially not when some of these guys make $30–40 mil a year just in trading.

THEO: So then why make it up?

CHARL [*indignant and frustrated*]: Who knows? Who knows, Theo? Why make anything up? It's what we keep coming back to.

THEO: So then you never thought Susanna was dangerous?

CHARL: I mean, at the time I did because, despite every-thing, I still believed most of what he said when he spoke.

MARQUETTE: I chalk the Susanna stuff up to a base of knowledge I didn't have. Because his conversations—one-sided conversations—were mostly about him tell-ing me things I didn't know and me questioning the information I already had. Despite my confusion, it still seemed like it was coming from a good place.

CHARL: Which is why I believed him about her that summer. He sent us that text pretty soon after we came back from Houston—

MARQUETTE: The one about them breaking up and her stealing his debit card and charging thirty-five grand at some boutique clothing store?

CAM: That's the one.

CHARL: It didn't happen. None of it was true. Ever.

MARQUETTE: Can we play under the assumption that it did for a minute?

CHARL: Why?

MARQUETTE: Just bear with me.

CHARL: Okay.

MARQUETTE: So, Susanna steals his debit card infor-mation. Mikey doesn't say how, right?

CHARL: Not to my recollection.

MARQUETTE: Just says that she stole his information and ran up a tab. We assume it's true now as we assumed it was true then. Why would Mikey then tell us to delete her from social media?

CAM: I mean, a scam is really the only thing I could think of.

THEO: Yeah, I was gonna say, some kind of scam where she, I dunno, somehow gets our information, I guess? From Facebook posts?

CHARL: Definitely not. She's a doctor, dude. How many doctors are spending their free time learning to mine data from social media?

THEO: I'd guess close to zero.

CHARL: Zero. Zero doctors, who are spending ten years post-grad to fucking save lives and help people are going to perform elaborate social media scams to get credit card information from their boyfriend's friends whom they've never met. Nothing about this makes sense. And look, guys. I agree, he's persuasive. He was. He called me one night and had me convinced she was hiding out outside of my place. I bolted my doors and kept my lights off. But it was all lies.

THEO: But there's literally no reason for that, man. It doesn't make sense.

CHARL: You're right, Theo. It doesn't make sense. It's the very definition of "insane."

MARQUETTE: It's sad, because we know the Sunnyside Mikey, the Austin Mikey, the version of him that was always there, which is why saying, out loud, everything that he said and did in Houston has been so hard to actually hear. Even now, it just doesn't jibe with who I thought he was.

CHARL: We have to come to admit that we were in an abusive relationship, and still might be, honestly. Where we take these nuggets of good, these wonderful memories of happy times, probably the best times in my life, and we use that—or used that—to give the negatives a pass. To say, in essence, "This isn't normal, he'll go back to normal one day," and we never give ourselves the option of adhering to the reality of the new normal.

CAM: That's very well said, Charl.

THEO: Yeah, dude.

MARQUETTE [*deadpan*]: No it's not.

CHARL [*laughing*]: Thanks, you guys. It's hard to say, you know?

CAM: Definitely.

THEO: That fall, the weekend he was supposed to come down, that was the weekend he was supposed to have a date with my friend, Leandra, right?

CAM: Yup. Same weekend as my birthday party.

THEO: Oh snap. Right! Because your party was Friday, and he was supposed to meet up with Leandra that Saturday.

CAM: And he didn't show up to either.

CHARL: That, for me, was the biggest sin.

MARQUETTE: The excuse?

CHARL: Missing Cam's party. We'd been planning it for months.

MARQUETTE: Oh, I was talking about the why.

CHARL: Right. I—look—I've had almost two years to figure out, diagram, that night, and my mind just kinda goes [*He makes the sound of an explosion and opens his balled-up fists near his head, mimicking an explosion itself.*]

THEO: I feel like such a fool.

CAM: Why?

THEO: I mean, the first thing I thought of when he told us, like, a week later, or whenever it was, when he "reemerged," was "oh shit, he almost died."

MARQUETTE: At this point, I was pretty skeptical of him, but don't feel bad, I thought the same thing.

CHARL: An avalanche? Guys. C'mon. He missed Cam's party. [*He motions to* THEO.] He stood up your friend on a date he planned with her and he tells us it's because he almost suffocated under some snow in Vermont?

CAM: I heard a little more than that.

CHARL: Really?

CAM: I heard that his cousin didn't know how to ski and veered off the path, and Mikey followed him into a snowbank to save him or something.

CHARL: Oh Jesus Christ.

CAM: The snow patrol was out there for half a day looking for them, but couldn't find them because they were buried, according to him.

THEO: He said he had hypothermia and just when he was about to pass out—

CHARL: Just when he was about to pass out, at the last minute, right? At the last minute, the patrol found them and pulled them to safety.

MARQUETTE: He said he was in a coma for a week.

CHARL: Bullshit.

CAM: Of course it's bullshit. He had his father call me like a day before he group chatted us. I get a phone call from a number I don't recognize, some 347 area code. And I'm like, "Um, hello?" And his dad, he—

CHARL: His "dad."

CAM: Whoever. It was some older guy like, "Hi, this is Mikey's father. I'm calling you because you were in his contacts list." Then he told me the same story, Mikey and his cousin were in Vermont for the weekend, skiing, there was an accident, the whole deal.

THEO: Leandra said she got a call from his dad, too.

CHARL: It's an attempt to legitimize illegitimacy.

THEO: Who else would have called them, though?

MARQUETTE: Maybe it *was* his dad, that doesn't mean his dad wasn't in on the lie.

CHARL: Yeah man. All lies.

THEO: And when he told us, I was terrified for him. I was imagining him jumping in after his cousin and, like, heroically holding onto him for warmth under a pile of snow, terrified, freezing—

CHARL: Dude, we met his cousin at the wedding. He is a very large man.

CAM: Close to two-fifty.

CHARL: Mikey's strong, but he's not that strong.

THEO: But what was your first reaction to his texts? Like, was I the only one who was imagining him hooked up to life support, tubes beeping or, like, wheezing, fuckin' doctors coming in, reading his charts, huddling in private, that kinda thing?

MARQUETTE: In the beginning, yeah, that's naturally where my mind went, but it collapses under the slightest bit of scrutiny.

THEO: Like…?

CHARL: Like, for one thing, this wasn't in the paper. Anywhere. No mention of this miraculous story in any paper. No news footage, no tweets, no Facebook posts. Nothing. It all just happened in the vacuum of his mind.

CAM: Did Leandra believe him?

THEO: Honestly, Leandra didn't know what to think. She didn't have any of the history that we all did, so I'm pretty sure she took him at face value.

MARQUETTE: But they didn't go on a date again?

THEO: No. They didn't go the first time—

MARQUETTE: Right.

THEO: I know what you're saying, though. No, they never went out again. But I went down to Houston to see him shortly after that.

CAM: Really?

THEO: Yeah. I had a conference down there and figured that I'd rather stay with him than at a Radisson. So I pocketed the per diem and stayed with him. Figured he needed someone at the moment, so soon after a breakup and everything he'd been through. It's hard being alone when you don't want to be.

CHARL: Dude.

THEO: He seemed really down when we spoke, and his affect got significantly brighter when I asked to stay over. Also, I thought it'd be a good chance for me to get some information from him, to find out what the fuck was going on, ya know?

MARQUETTE: I remember this. It didn't go well.

THEO: It didn't *not* go well, but it wasn't what I expected. I texted him when I was downstairs, and he buzzed me in. On the way over, he shot me a text and it said… hold up. [*He pulls out his phone, unlocks it, and opens the messages app.*]

CAM: Didn't he cover his walls with cray paper or something because the doctors said it would help with
the post-traumatic stress?

THEO: Right. So, he said, [*He reads from his phone.*] "Hey buddy, so glad you're coming. Just so you know, my place is gonna look a little weird. Everything's covered in black. Doctor's orders (LOL, the irony is enticing, I know). I'll explain when you get here."

MARQUETTE: It said, "Doctor's orders"?

THEO [*showing* MARQUETTE *his phone*]: And he was right. The entire place was blanketed in—

MARQUETTE: Blankets.

THEO: I guess? [*He puts his phone back in his pocket.*] It was black. Posters were covered. Mirrors.

CHARL: Wasn't the lock off his door, too?

THEO: Oh shit, yeah. The lock *was* off his door.

CAM: I don't remember this.

CHARL: Yeah, didn't he say someone broke into his place to access his files?

CAM: What files?

CHARL: *The* files, Cam.

CAM: Am I missing something?

CHARL: There were no files, man.

THEO: He told me he hired a bodyguard.

CAM: There was a bodyguard there?

THEO: No.

CAM: Um—

THEO: He said the bodyguard was across the way, watching the apartment.

MARQUETTE: How did I forget this?

THEO: Yeah. I went to look out the window—the shades were drawn, and the venetian blinds were twisted—so I tried to open the curtains and he yelled at me to… well, not yelled, but shouted to me not to go near the window because then they'd, like, know he was home.

CAM: Who?

THEO: I dunno. Them?

CHARL: Holy mother.

CAM: So the bodyguard was watching the place that was completely covered—

THEO: Yup.

CAM: —where no light could get in—

THEO: Uh huh.

CAM: —and no one could actually see inside?

THEO: That's right.

CAM: Bruh.

THEO: I was actually concerned that someone was gonna try and break in while I was there.

CHARL: Dude.

THEO: I asked him about it. The darkness, I mean. He said it swaddled him, that it calmed him down and he didn't really even need to sleep any more because of it.

CHARL: What?

THEO: He said he didn't want to take anti-anxieties, so they recommended minimizing light once or twice a week.

CHARL: That seems like the opposite advice a doctor would give.

CAM: Right.

CHARL: Vitamin D is in sunlight. It affects mood. It's why going outside feels good even when you feel bad.

THEO: I know. Or at least I thought I did. If two doctors said that—

CHARL: Two?

THEO: Well, the other doctor and him.

CHARL: Right.

THEO: If two doctors gave that advice, maybe I was wrong, I dunno.

CHARL: No, man.

THEO: He also said that he couldn't use technology on the weekends because they were monitoring his calls.

CHARL: What?

MARQUETTE: Who was?

THEO: The people hired to spy on him? The university, I guess.

CHARL: And you didn't "nope" right the fuck outta there?

CAM: Jesus.

THEO: No, dude. If it was you guys, I woulda done the same thing.

CHARL [*sighing*]: Theo. There was a clear pattern emerging at this point, and—

THEO: Yeah, but patterns only emerge when you step back from them. Like a mosaic.

MARQUETTE: Or a Magic Eye.

THEO: Wanted to go with the less-dated reference, but yeah.

CHARL: Dude—

THEO [*frustrated*]: Come on, man. You were still talking to him at this point. You didn't cut him out. Please don't act like you knew something we all didn't.

CHARL: Honestly, I stopped talking to him right after my wedding. If you go back, you'll see I just never responded to the group texts. It was just easier to let things play out as they did then try to tell a lifelong friend that you no longer want to be around him. If he continued to be unreliable and untrustworthy, we'd all just kind of wise up to it and he'd know that he messed up. If he came around and started being the same person we knew—or thought we knew—then I'd be able to slowly re-navigate those waters.

THEO: You wanted to have it both ways.

CHARL: Pretty much, yeah. It may not have been the most mature thing to do, or the most responsible, but it was the easiest considering the circumstances.

THEO: I *will* say that when I was there, it was hard for me to talk earnestly with him about what was going on. I wanted to keep the conversation light and fun and… I dunno, I wanted it to be a return to form. I thought that maybe if he felt like things were how they used to be then they'd be how they used to be again.

MARQUETTE: Do you guys think that if you had that diffi-cult conversations with him, if he heard from you in a straightforward and honest way—

THEO: Maybe? I can't really say.

CHARL: I pussed out.

MARQUETTE: You didn't puss out. You did what you thought was right at the time given the evidence you had. No one faults you for that.

THEO: I think you pussed out.

CHARL: You pussed out too, puss.

THEO: I did.

CAM: Well, I didn't.

MARQUETTE: What'd you say?

CAM: I called him up, told him he needed to get his shit together, that he was fucking up. I stressed his drunk driving charge because that shit was crazy to me.

THEO: But it didn't have any impact.

CAM: I mean, it did, but just not the impact that we want-ed, right? We wanted, you said, and I agree, we wanted a return to normal. He didn't want that. Whatever it was, it wasn't that.

MARQUETTE: He *did* apologize to all of us, and it seemed like things were gonna get better.

THEO: Yeah, he sent that text while I was there. He apolo-gized for just about everything. For ghosting. For being weird. For not showing up. For all of it. Said he was going through a lot. Talked about trauma. Going to therapy. Told me more about growing up, how his mom was never around, how his dad was pretty much absent, too. So he stuck his head in books and kinda just pushed through childhood emotions because that's what you were "supposed to do."

MARQUETTE: We never met his mom, did we?

THEO: Nah, just his dad.

CHARL: He was, uh, not very nice.

MARQUETTE: No.

THEO: But we had a nice time while I was there. We played some Madden, ordered a pizza. I fell asleep on his couch and I woke up with blankets on me and a note on the table. It was cute. I left shortly afterwards.

CAM: But he kept ghosting.

CHARL: He kept ghosting.

MARQUETTE: The problem was that he was unreliable, and every new thing that happened was, um, it wasn't excused, but, explained with an understanding of "oh, that's just Mikey." Which sucks, because I never want to think of my friends as being just one thing or just another, but we were getting used to that being what we accepted as part of our new friendship.

THEO: What was the breaking point for you all?

MARQUETTE: You mean aside from murdering his wife?

CAM: It's a pretty big aside.

THEO: There's just so much more.

CHARL: There's *so* much more, dude. The hotel, his second arrest, the fucking—dude, he didn't show up to your wedding. Another wedding he missed.

THEO: I know.

CHARL: Can I propose something?

THEO: Go ahead.

CHARL: One hour. [*He looks at his watch.*] It's 11:04 now. Let's go get another drink. Let's go for a walk. Let's clear our heads and talk about anything but Mikey, because there's, yeah, there's a lot. It's just a lot, man, and I need some time to breathe.

CAM: That's fair.

THEO: One hour.

CHARL: One hour.

MARQUETTE: I'll go get some beers.

—The CURTAIN falls

ACT III

12:14 A.M.

When the CURTAIN *rises,* THEO *is standing downstage. Behind him,* MARQUETTE, CAM, *and* CHARL *silently take turns playing pinball. They laugh with one another and stand around, joking and drinking beers.* THEO *looks back at them and then looks at the audience.*

THEO [*holding a mug of beer*]: It wasn't until Marquette got up that I realized how enveloped our little table had become. People stood sentinel around us, painting our discussion with a discordant chorus of voices. And though I'd assume none of their conversations were as important, I'd never really know. We chatted, shared pictures and memes and YouTube videos, though the latter were difficult to hear amidst the clamor. But most importantly, we laughed. We laughed and laughed and laughed and laughed. We shared inside jokes, jokes that dated back two, ten, twenty years. Phrases that, even now, written out or spoken aloud, look and sound ridiculous, esoteric, dumb, incongruent, almost embarrassing. But to us, they're magic. Like a batch of secret phrases known to no one else.

MARQUETTE, CAM, *and* CHARL *finish playing and make their way back to the table.*

The true beauty of them is that they're not planned. You don't sit down and map out a discussion that is peppered with callbacks. You just callback because you can, because it's as natural as breathing. It's its own form of life, in a way.

THEO *walks upstage and joins them, putting his beer down on the table.*

Okay. It's about 12:15. This place does last call at 1.

MARQUETTE: More rum runner?

CHARL AND CAM: No.

MARQUETTE: Joking.

THEO: Just trying to give us a time frame here.

CHARL: It's been about an hour.

THEO: Exactly an hour.

CHARL: Actually, it's been ten minutes over an hour.

THEO: You tryin'a get a frying pan to the face?

CHARL: Dude.

CAM: Oh fuck.

THEO: Look, I'm not the one who actually did it.

MARQUETTE: According to Mikey, neither was he.

THEO: Did any of you actually see the affidavit?

CHARL, CAM, AND MARQUETTE: No.

THEO: Nah, me neither.

CAM: He called me. I was—this must have been shortly after you saw him, Theo, because I was in the airport on the way to Alabama for the Clemson game.

MARQUETTE: What'd he say to you?

CAM: Said he'd just got outta jail—

CHARL: Again.

CAM: —again. And wanted to explain what happened before the rumors started.

CHARL: Okay, right, I remember this.

CAM: He said that he and Susanna were cooking at his place and there was an argument about something. She was yelling—according to him—that he's no good, that he's not supportive, shit like that. And he turned around to face her, the frying pan slipped from his hand and hit her in the arm.

CHARL: "Slipped."

CAM: That's what he said. That it slipped from his hand and hit her in the arm, leaving a bruise or a burn or some kind of mark on her that she used as evidence when she called the cops six days later.

CHARL: It was six days?

CAM: That's what he said. That's why they briefly broke up. Again, I haven't seen the police report, and I likely never will, but he claims that's why they let him out of jail. No evidence.

CHARL: I didn't remember that.

THEO: I still don't know how they got back together. Like, how do you get back together with someone who called the cops on you?

CHARL: You don't.

CAM: Well, *you* don't. People definitely do. My mom, for example, she—look, when you're desperate for love, you accept less than what you're worth.

THEO: Your mom?

CAM: Before online dating was a thing, she would send away videotapes. Like, you remember those, what were they, those personal ads but—

MARQUETTE: Your mom did Video Dating?

CAM: I didn't find out till later—now she thinks it's hilarious—but yeah, she would sit in the living room and just be like, "Hello, my name is Harriette. I'm thirty-nine years old and I want—"

CHARL [*interrupting*]: "…to find a man who will sit on my face."

EVERYONE *laughs*.

CAM: But I guess the point is, if you're desperate, you kind of convince yourself that the person in front of you is the one you need because, otherwise, they wouldn't be in front of you.

THEO: Mikey was never needy, though.

CAM: Hard to classify, right? You can have the need for love, like that internal pulling for validation through another person without ever classifying it that way. Mikey was cavalier about most things; it doesn't mean he didn't feel any kind of yearning.

CHARL: Cam, didn't you and Martina get drinks with Susanna?

CAM: Yeah, about two weeks before they got married.

MARQUETTE: I forgot that you guys met her.

CAM: Yeah.

MARQUETTE: And he wasn't there?

CAM: Nah, she was in Austin visiting family, remember? Mikey reached out to us on group text, asked if we could meet her for drinks.

CHARL: So what happened?

CAM: She told us how awful she felt for what she did to Mikey and how she wishes she could take it all back and, like, it was just a very strange… [*He sighs.*] It was weird because it felt like I couldn't trust anything either of them had said. And she contradicted a lot of what he said. That she did mess up by taking his debit card, that she had never heard about him being buried in snow, that she did call the cops because he hit her with a frying pan but that she admitted she may have overreacted in the moment. I wasn't sure if she was being manipulated by him into believing what she said, if she actually believed it, or what the truth really was.

THEO: She apologized for taking his debit card? She admitted that?

CAM: Tacitly. She said she apologized for "stealing from him" and that she didn't know what would possess her to betray his trust. She was telling us she didn't deserve him, and it was kinda scary, honestly, because I didn't know what kind of person I was talking to.

CHARL: Damn.

CAM: This was my final effort to try and understand who he was, who she was, and who they were together.

THEO: Yeah, but it's like trying to understand a tornado by staring through the eye.

CHARL: Yes. That's exactly what it's like, Theo.

CAM: After the dinner though, maybe a day or two, he called me.

MARQUETTE: Late night?

CAM: Around eleven. And I knew that it would end up being a long conversation so I just kinda braced for it.

Truthfully, I was happy he was reaching out, and I figured it would be a recap of the night, what we thought of Susanna, all the normal, regular stuff normal, regular people do after their friends meet their girlfriend.

CHARL: Say Cameron, you, uh, you used the phrase "normal, regular" there twice.

CAM: Don't use my full government name.

EVERYONE *laughs*.

He was convinced I was spreading lies.

THEO: What?

CAM: It was a long conversation.

CHARL: I bet. When you go around telling people that you wrote songs for Fabolous and that you had dinner with Ari Fleischer it's—

THEO: What?

MARQUETTE: Who?

CHARL: Yeah guys. You didn't know this? He said Ari Fleischer—the former press secretary for the Bush administration—was a family friend and that he came over to his place for a meal.

THEO: Get the fuck out of here.

MARQUETTE: When did he tell you this?

CHARL: Oh man, like, a year ago, two years ago.

THEO: Ari Fleischer?

CHARL: Ari Fleischer.

MARQUETTE: How did you react?

CHARL: I mean, I went along with it, disbelievingly. You can't convince someone who's convinced of something to be unconvinced of that thing, even if it didn't happen. It's why it's hard to verify anything he's ever said. He's an unreliable narrator in his own story, for Christ sakes.

THEO: Like when he said that they made him chief of surgery before they could legally announce it because they didn't want to draw attention t—

CHARL [*interrupting*]: He was never the chief of surgery.

MARQUETTE: He was not.

THEO [*resignedly*]: Goddammit.

CHARL: So when did he leave Baylor?

MARQUETTE: Wait, I wanna hear more about your conversation with him, Cam.

CAM: What? Oh, yeah. Well, to sum it up, he said he didn't like that I was spreading lies and—

CHARL: But you wer—

CAM [*interrupting* CHARL *by holding up his hand*]: He wanted to understand why I didn't believe him. So I told him, I told him just what I've told you guys. That he's unreliable. That he's non-responsive. That he didn't value our time as friends and that I thought he cared more about his status as a person than he did the relationships he had.

MARQUETTE: Wow.

CAM: And he apologized.

CHARL: Again.

CAM: Yeah. He said he understood, said it's why he quit his job and was pursuing his passion with politics and that he wanted to make the world better on a larger level. "Influence change on a grand scale," I remember him saying. Which is noble, right? It's a noble thing to do and say and to believe.

CHARL: If it were real.

CAM: He told me he got a whole bunch of investors in his company, and—

THEO: What? Wait.

MARQUETTE: What company?

CAM [*shrugging*]: He knew them from Baylor, he said. There were millions of dollars promised and that he's busier than ever but that he's more professionally satisfied. He seemed happy and, though erratic, sincere. He ended with an apology and asked me if I liked going to [*He pauses very slightly.*] Vegas.

CHARL *sighs*.

He forwarded me that confirmation email with a weekend stay for me and Martina.

MARQUETTE: That whole thing still doesn't make sense to me.

CHARL [*to* CAM]: You went to leave and they made you pay, is that what happened?

CAM: Kind of. The front desk told me that the credit card used for payment had been removed from the reservation.

CHARL: That's so fucked up.

CAM: Yeah. They wouldn't let me leave until I paid, so I withdrew $16,000 from my bank account at the ATM. Left me with twenty-seven bucks to my name. Motherfucker.

MARQUETTE: And those fees are through the roof.

CHARL: When compared to $16,000, though, it's

MARQUETTE: No, I mean, I know, I know.

CAM: And then I texted him and called him and emailed him. Nothing. No answer. No response. No "read" notification… for months.

CHARL: When did he end up contacting you? Was it the summer?

CAM: Nah, a little before that, but it was all bullshit. Said that he kept trying to Venmo me but it kept being denied. That his assets were tied up in his business, so he couldn't use PayPal, which was his business account.

He even said he sent me a check, but I never saw that shit.

THEO: He did that shit for no reason, too. Like, what do you gain from that?

CHARL: Power.

THEO: What? What power do you need to have over friends who you've known for almost thirty years?

CHARL: Power's irrational, man. I can't explain it. But there's some element to his thought processes that led him to believe that this was okay.

THEO: But there's always a gain tied to scams. There's something at the end of it. Monetary or social or whatever, but at the end of this is just loneliness and anger.

CAM: Maybe that's what he wanted.

THEO: Who would want that?

CAM: Maybe he wanted to break ties with us but couldn't figure out how to do it.

CHARL: So you run a scam on your friends that costs one of them almost twenty grand? No, man. Never chalk up to malice what you can chalk up to stupidity.

MARQUETTE: He's never been a dumb guy.

CHARL: Social stupidity. Mix that with stubbornness and inability to process apologies properly—

THEO: He apologized, though. Multiple times.

CHARL: And look at what happened as a result.

CAM: Nah-ting.

CHARL: Exactly. Dude, empty words ring hollow for a reason. He went through the motions of apologizing because that's what you're supposed to do, not because that's what he wanted to do.

CAM: Like a fucking sociopath.

MARQUETTE: You know, we've been getting down on ourselves now for "not seeing it coming." But you have to remember, in between all of these bullshit events, there was calm, and there were elements of him trying to be better. Charl, he flew you to Houston in a helicopter to catch a Rockets game.

CHARL: He did. And that's insane!

CAM: That's who he became, though, Charl. It was the logical next step for someone who always threw his money around. If I were making a graph, it would be a direct line from drinks to front-row seats to a weekend in Vegas to helicopter. And don't get me wrong, all these stockpiled lies: the arrests, Ari Fleischer. Fucking Fabolous. Insider trading. Skiing—

THEO: Gigi Hadid.

CAM: They're too much to really make sense of. And that's not to mention stuff we might not even know about.

MARQUETTE: I always had this notion that it was all a big misunderstanding. That nothing he said was lies, it was just shitty follow-through. Because it's what I knew about him. That shit's hard to supplant.

THEO: Whose decision was it to not have another wedding? Had to be his, right?

CHARL: Could be.

THEO: After they eloped, he started calling me at one or two in the morning. And because it had been so long since I heard from him regularly, I'd always answer, and he'd talk and talk and talk for like three hours straight, telling me about the connections he's making and how hard he's been working to get his new business off the ground and how I'd make a great spokesperson for the company and how all of that would come with a book deal and an apartment and it's like… he was turning sentences into knots, untying and retying them while I struggled to follow along.

CHARL: Cocaine will do that.

THEO: He was on coke?

CHARL: It's pretty obvious.

MARQUETTE: Again, we don't know this. He never told us he used coke.

CHARL: Why would he?

MARQUETTE: He told us he smoked. We drank together.

CHARL: Different, man. There's a level of social acceptability, and it's tiered, usually tailored to friends. If your friends aren't drug users, then drug use is seen as taboo.

CAM: It's likely he was on coke, but we don't know he was on coke. If we're breaking down what he did factually, we can't include speculation.

CHARL: Okay. Well, we know they got married at the Justice of the Peace. It was his first Instagram post in, like, five years.

THEO: You know the one before it? [*He takes out his phone and opens it to Instagram.*]

CHARL: No.

THEO: It's us.

CHARL: Really?

THEO: Yeah dude.

CHARL: Where's it from?

THEO: It's us in Austin. [*He scrolls, then passes his phone to* CHARL.] See?

CHARL: Oh man. I loved this picture. [*He shows* MARQUETTE *and* CAM *the photo on the phone before handing it back to* THEO.]

MARQUETTE: I think we all did. I still do.

CAM: I can't look at it the same.

THEO [*putting his phone away*]: It's like seeing a picture of joy right before tragedy.

CAM: It's hard, right? It's hard to take what was a happy memory and see it for anything other than what it became. So I don't really know.

CHARL: Right.

MARQUETTE: And how long after he was married did he… you know…

CAM: Two months.

CHARL: Portia tried to do a google search on him shortly after they got married.

THEO: What did she find?

CHARL: Nothing, really. Just an announcement about their wedding in the Free Press Houston. She was pissed that we didn't get an invite. Her reasoning, and it's one I agree with, was that we're not the ones who fucked up. Inviting us to his wedding would have been a big step towards a true apology.

CAM: Another big step would've been getting me my goddamned money back.

CHARL: Pretty much.

THEO: Would you guys have gone?

CAM: No. Fuck him.

MARQUETTE: Probably not, no.

CHARL: No. But that doesn't mean that we shouldn't have been invited. It's the principal of it all, man. If he wanted to still be friends the way he said, a simple gesture like that is the bare minimum.

THEO: Right.

CHARL: You'd have gone, Theo?

THEO: Probably not, no. I'd want to, but it would have been jumping into the deep end when I'd rather have just put my toes in, you know? I'm actually kind of glad we weren't invited though, considering everything that came afterwards.

MARQUETTE: What does that newspaper article say again?

THEO: Which one?

MARQUETTE: The one about the murder.

THEO: There's a bunch of 'em.

MARQUETTE: Just read the first result.

THEO [*taking out his phone*]: Alright. [*He types into his phone. There is a momentary silence of anticipation.*] Okay. Here's one. From the *Chronicle*. [*He reads the article from his phone to the group.*]: "One day after a Houston woman was reported missing, her husband has become the prime suspect in her murder. His current whereabouts are unknown.

"Susanna D'Orio, 28, was reported missing on Friday around 8:30 p.m. after she stopped responding to text messages and phone calls from friends, Texas State Police said. Police issued a Missing Adult Alert for her on

Saturday afternoon, and by Saturday evening, she was found dead in the home she shared with her husband."

CHARL: Jesus.

THEO [*continuing to read*]: "Police said Michael D'Orio, 35, of Houston, was identified as a suspect in the slaying. The Houston Police Department says they are prepared to charge him with first-degree murder and possession of a deadly weapon. 'We are searching diligently in and around the Houston area for the person of interest,' said Police Chief Robert McHorry. 'While we have a number of leads, the community should share any information available. As a father, I want this violent criminal off the streets.'"

CAM: How long ago was this?

THEO [*scrolling on his phone*]: Um… about a month.

MARQUETTE: A month?

CAM *laughs derisively*

CHARL [*muttering in anger*]: Unbelievable. This is unbelievable. I'm so angry. I thought I was okay, I really did, but hearing this, man… [*He trails off then exhales.*]

THEO [*continuing to read*]: "According to the Houston Police Department, the investigation revealed that the homicide was the result of repeated blunt force trauma to the head. Police later found blood and strands of D'Orio's hair attached to a wine bottle, which is believed to be the murder weapon, in the couple's refrigerator."

CHARL: God. Can we just stop, please?

MARQUETTE: Yeah, I'm sorry for asking. I don't think I need to hear this again.

CAM *sips the last of his vodka soda slurping air through the straw. He sighs.*

There is a stillness as the men contemplate what they've heard once again.

THEO [*putting his phone away*]: So how do we come to grips with this?

CHARL: What do you mean?

THEO: How do we say out loud, "Our friend is a murderer"?

CAM: Whoa. He's not my friend.

THEO: Sure. You know what I mean. How do—what do we—do we just never bring him up again?

CHARL: I'd like that option, yeah.

THEO: It's kinda hard for me to do that. You go back with someone thirty years, you can't just photoshop them out of the memories.

CAM: To be honest, it's real easy for me. I just use generic terms like "my friends" or, if for some reason there's a story that needs to be told about him, I'll say, "some dude" or "this guy we all knew." No reason to bring his story into yours.

CHARL: Theo, I recommend today be the last day we speak his name.

THEO: Quette?

MARQUETTE: I don't really bring him up to anyone outside of you guys. There's no reason to.

CHARL: What possible reason could you have for… and now—

CAM: Especially now.

CHARL: *Especially* now. This isn't something—or someone—you should be even wanting to associate yourself with. Do you want the fucking cops calling your house again, man? What sense does that make?

THEO: No, no, I get that. I really do.

CHARL [*after a short pause*]: But?

THEO: Maybe there's no but. I guess… I guess it goes back to that discussion we had years ago—and earlier, too—can you separate the art from the artist? Can we take the Mikey we knew and appreciate that time for what it was knowing that we were creating all these wonderful memories with someone who would end up murdering his fucking wife?

CAM: I mean, I can't. Except for today, when I look back on my time in Sunnyside, in Austin, it's with you guys.

He doesn't even factor in. Like a faceless person in a dream.

CHARL: Completely agree.

THEO: But what I think about is: what if I reached out more? What if I forced him to get help?

CHARL: You can't think like that.

THEO: It's what I would have needed.

CAM: Sadly, man, this woulda happened no matter what. He was a train on a track and we had no ability—none of us—to move that lever and divert that train.

MARQUETTE [*to* THEO]: Are you crying?

THEO [*wiping away tears*]: Yeah, I'm sorry. I'm just… this is hard, guys. It's really hard to cover up something beautiful with something ugly. What we have together is so rare. It's so hard to find, and we found it. Twice. We found each other twice. And now it's ruined. It's stained. It's not the same. I still pass by these remnants of us in Austin. They're constant reminders of what we had. And when I see them, it's hard not to think about Mikey. That's probably why it's so hard for me to let this go.

The lights flicker, then raise up to three-quarters brightness.

[*He sniffles and chuckles.*] Last call.

MARQUETTE: I'm good.

CAM: Yeah, me too.

MARQUETTE: No one says you have to forget about him, Theo, but it's tempering expectations. It's recognizing that we all had the time of our lives when we were all together, appreciating that in the capsule of time in which it existed. It's getting drunk knowing you're going to have a hangover but drinking anyway because that shit's fun.

CAM: Spoken like an alcoholic.

EVERYONE *laughs*.

THEO: Should we have known?

CHARL: No.

CAM: If we should have known, then every single person in his life should have known.

MARQUETTE: Yeah, dude, sometimes you just… don't.

THEO: That's… I dunno, that's unsatisfying. It's…

CHARL: There's no mystery left, man.

THEO: I mean, they don't know where he is.

CHARL: Sure. But that's not ours to solve. And quite frankly, the less we have to do with it the better.

THEO: And you don't think he's gonna come looking for us?

CAM: Hell no. I'd turn his ass in in a heartbeat.

MARQUETTE: Yup.

CHARL: You wouldn't?

THEO: No, no, I would. Just checking, I guess. It's just—

MARQUETTE: There's a loss, man. It's profound, and it's something we will all have with us—and Susanna, fuck, dude, and her family, I can't even imagine…

CHARL: There's no one to blame but Mikey and I learned a long time ago that it's damaging to start looking inward when the problem exists outside of you.

THEO [*after a moment's thought*]: Yeah. Okay. Yeah, that's well said.

CHARL [*after a short pause*]: I think we should get going.

CAM: Are you guys staying with your folks?

MARQUETTE, THEO, AND CHARL: Yeah.

CAM: I'll get us an Uber.

THEO: It's okay. I'm gonna walk. It's only a couple blocks.

The men stand up and shake hands; they hug. MARQUETTE, CAM, *and* CHARL *exit stage right.* THEO *walks to center stage and speaks to the audience.*

So I walked home, after the goodbyes and the promises to see each other again and the one last laugh at something stupid. I walked down these streets, the ones that look exactly the same, but feel like using a second language after a long absence, like riding a bicycle, the "and yet…" portion of the familiar. Red bricks, staggered, held up the buildings that have changed names who knows how many times since they were built. They flaked off like talcum powder under my nails as my finger followed the track of layered concrete holding them in place. It was rough, calloused, cracked, imperfect; I rubbed it against my thumb, smoothing out the creases in my finger until, days later, it would be like they were never there in the first place. *[He turns around and walks downstage towards the exit, stage right.]*

CURTAIN

www.ingramcontent.com/pod-product-compliance
Lightning Source LLC
Chambersburg PA
CBHW031632130726
47900CB00019B/2591